MW01173302

MAD HATTER STATIONERIES

www.madht.co

Scan me for more books
Madht.co

Made in the USA
Middletown, DE
10 September 2024

60760401R00057